Stains 5/2/2014 - AM

IRON MAN™ VS TITANIUM MAN™

Based on the Marvel comic book series Iron Man
Adapted by Clarissa S. Wong
Illustrated by Ramon Bachs *and* Hi-Fi Design

Published by Marvel Press, an imprint of Disney Book Group. No part of this book may be reproduced or transmitted in any form or by any means, electronic or mechanical, including photocopying, recording, or by any information storage and retrieval system, without written permission from the publisher.

For information address Marvel Press, 114 Fifth Avenue, New York, New York 10011-5690.
Printed in the United States of America
First Edition
1 3 5 7 9 10 8 6 4 2
G658-7729-4-13046
ISBN 978-1-4231-5469-3

marvelkids.com

New York

SUSTAINABLE FORESTRY INITIATIVE
Certified Chain of Custody
Promoting Sustainable Forestry
www.sfiprogram.org
SFI-01415
The SFI label applies to the text stock

Boris Bulliski wanted to be the greatest inventor in the world. But the world was more impressed with Iron Man than with Boris's inventions. We'll see how invincible the "man of iron" truly is, Boris thought.

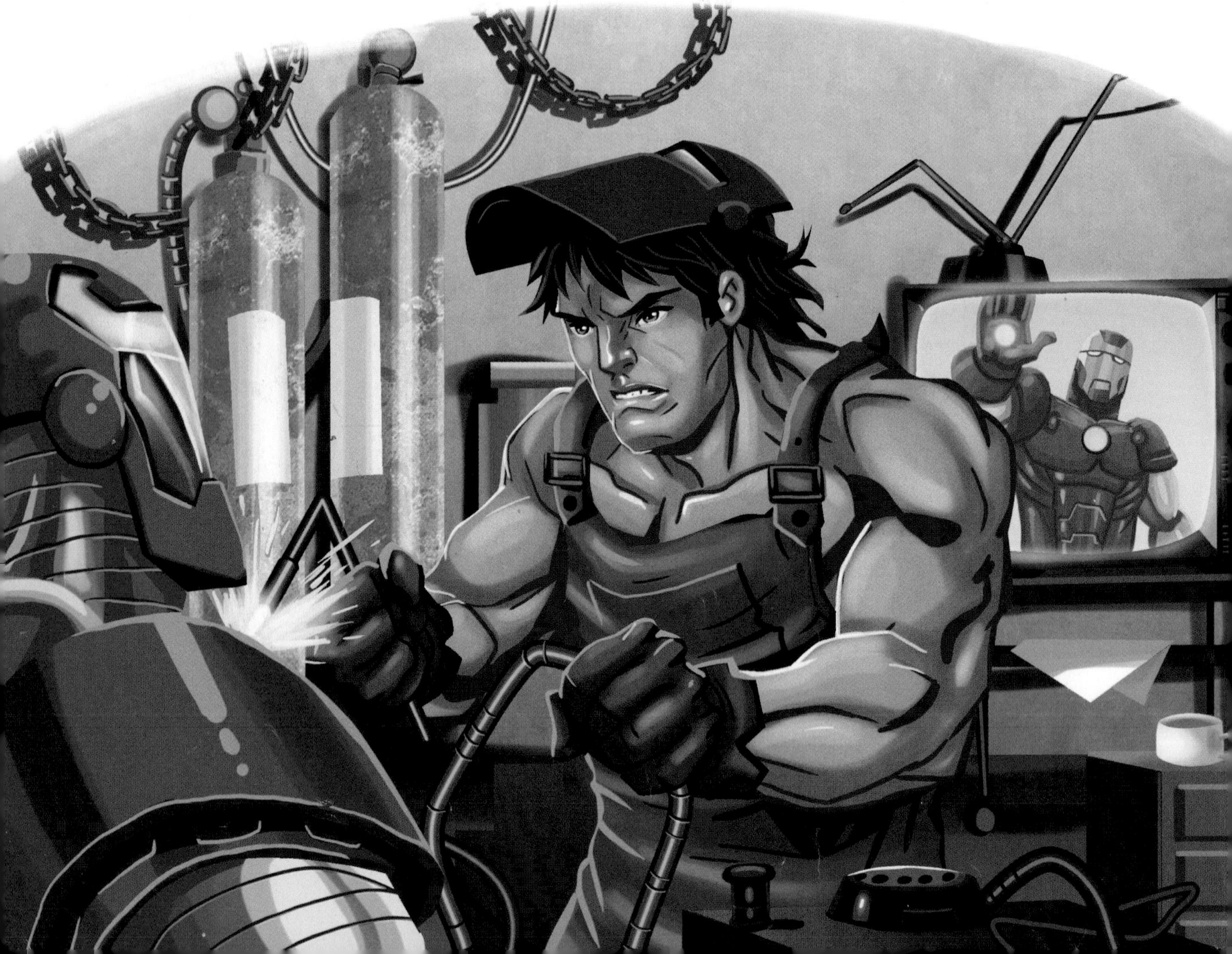

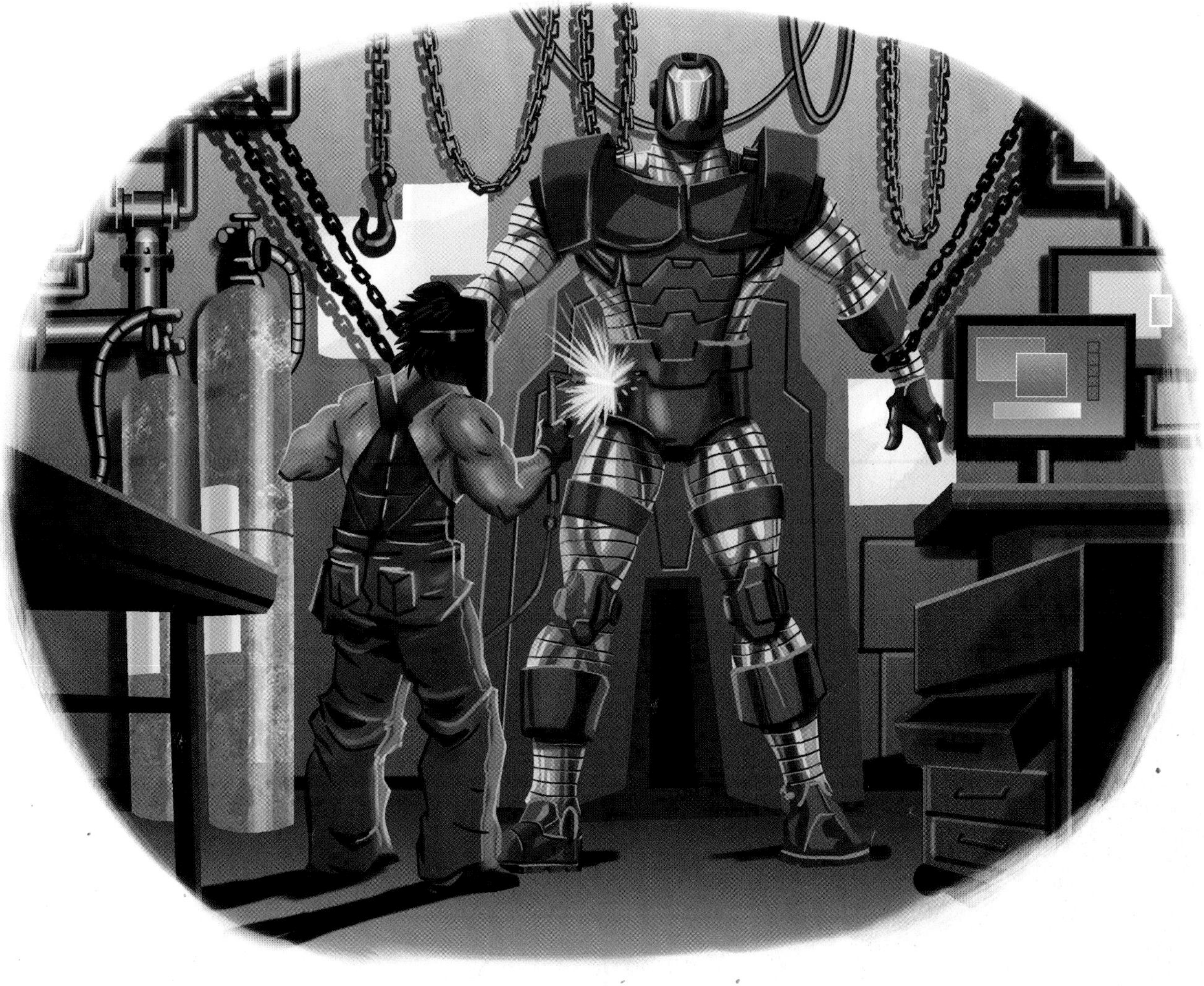

Boris was very proud of his latest invention, a suit made of the **powerful metal titanium!** Boris wanted to prove his invention was better than Iron Man's.

Tony Stark was watching the news in Stark Tower with his friends Pepper Potts and Happy Hogan. He was surprised to see that a mysterious character known as **"Titanium Man"** was challenging Iron Man. **"Well, Iron Man never backs down from a challenge,"** Tony said casually.

Tony was a little worried. Recently, he had tried to upgrade his repulsor rays. But there were still a few glitches. His **"fire blast"** upgrade used up a dangerous amount of energy. But this challenge wasn't supposed to be dangerous—or so he thought.

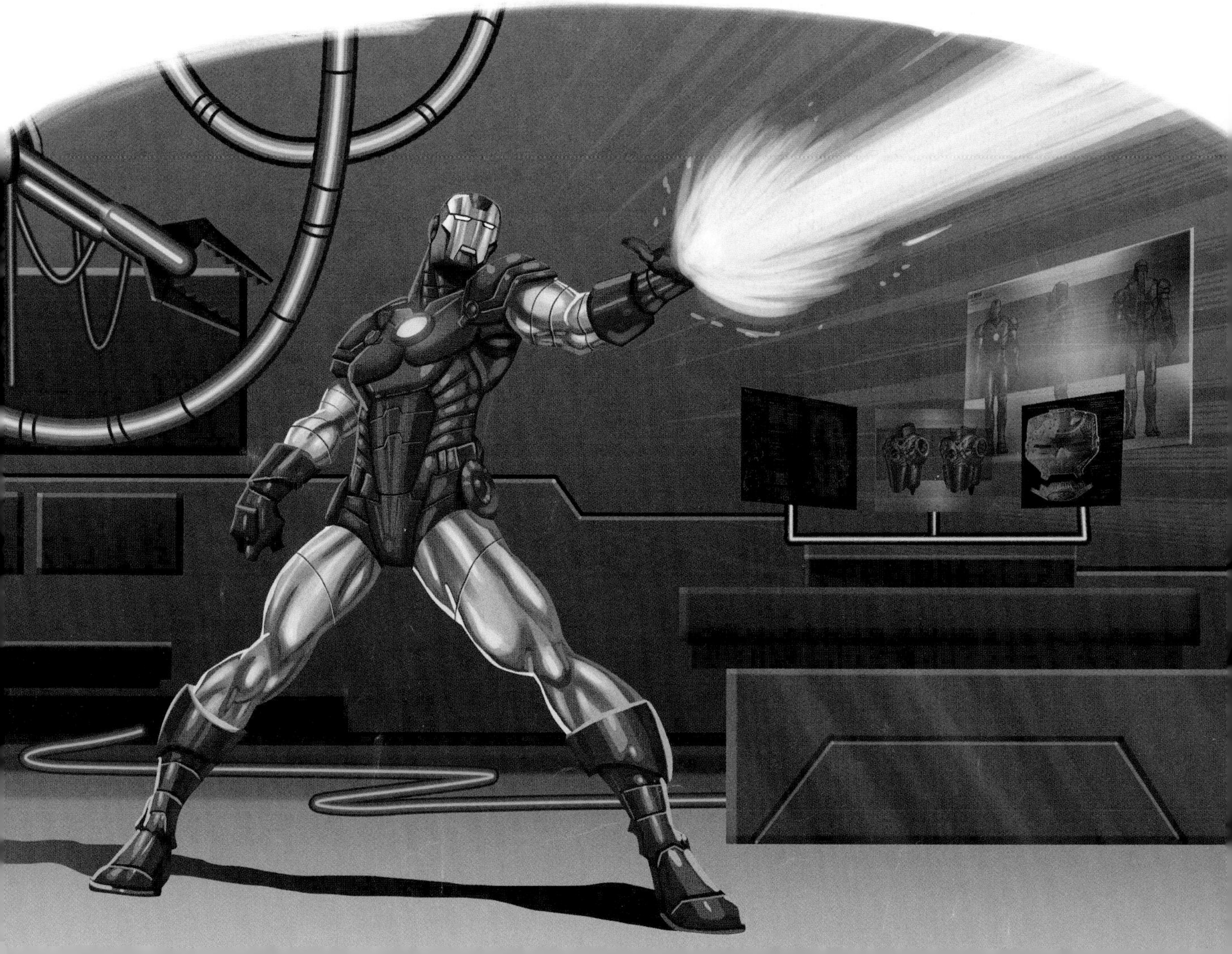

Iron Man was curious to finally meet his opponent. When Titanium Man arrived, Tony was shocked. He was **twice Iron Man's size!**

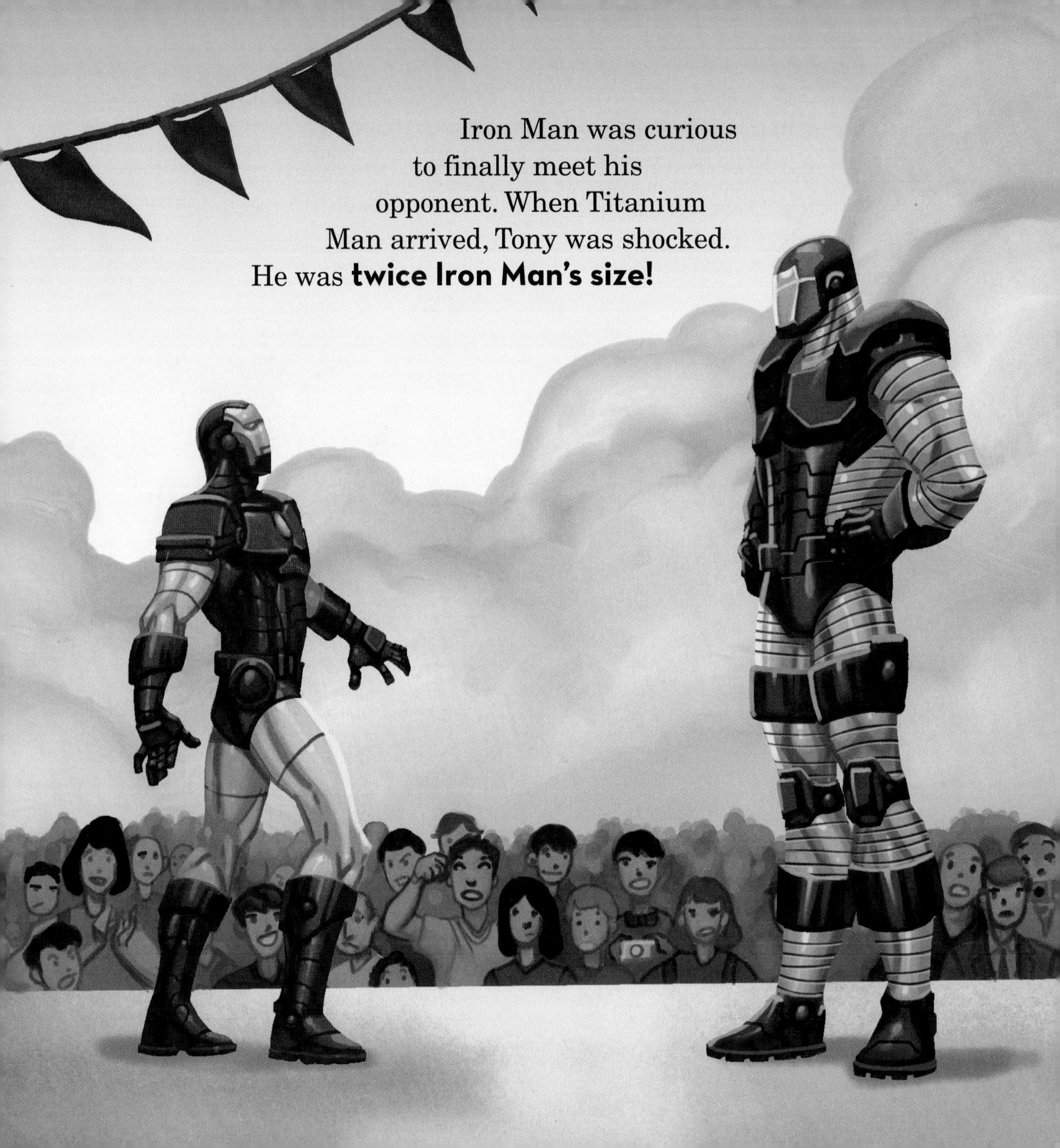

The first part of the challenge was to see who could lift an enormous boulder first. Iron Man slowly walked up to the large boulder and lifted it as high as his knees. The audience cheered loudly for the Armored Avenger.

Now, it was Titanium Man's turn. He picked up the stone as if it were nothing! He held the rock high above his head.

To everyone's surprise,
Titanium Man threw the rock
directly at Iron Man. Iron Man quickly
darted out of danger. "Hey, be careful, buddy,"
Tony warned.

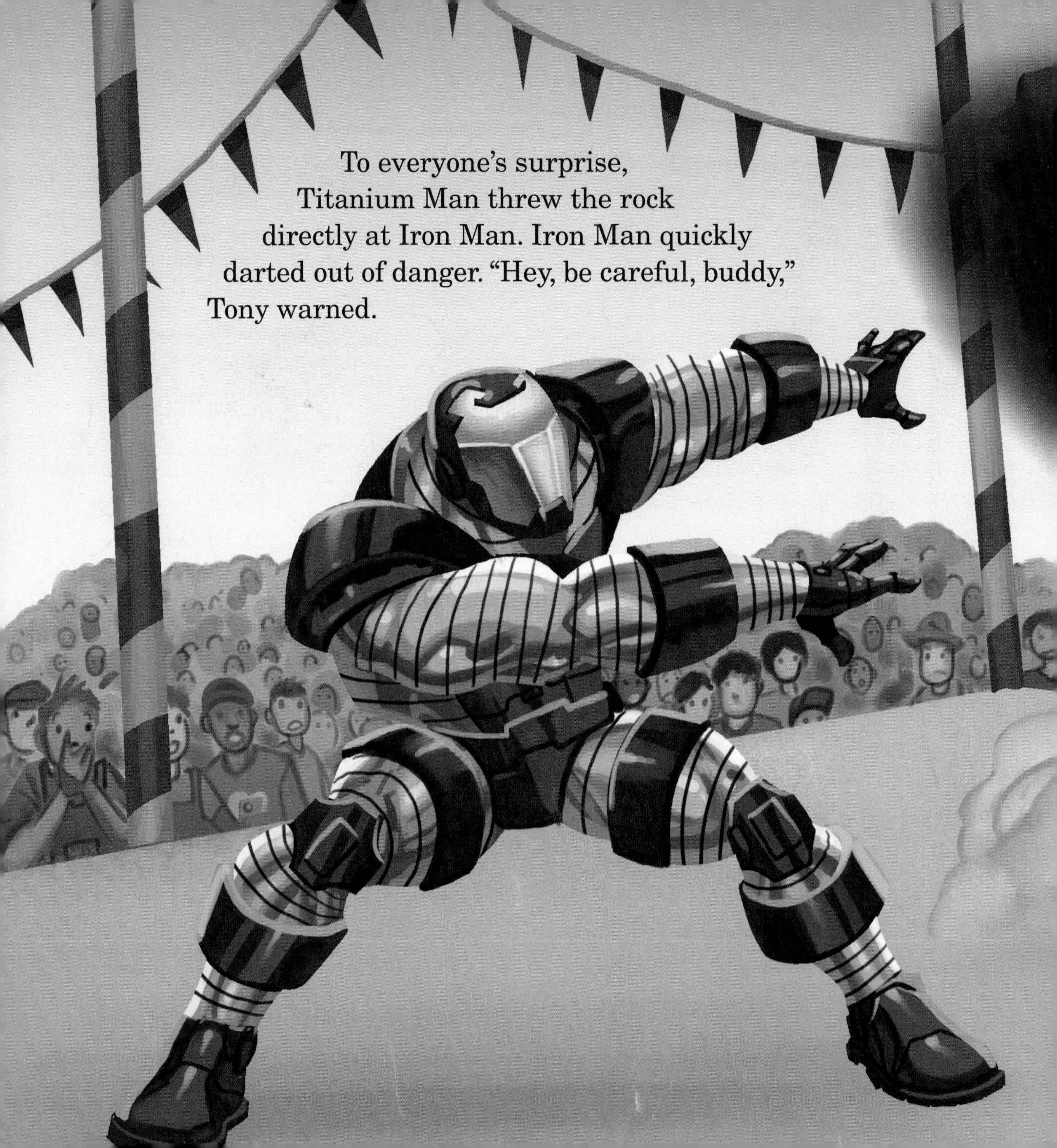

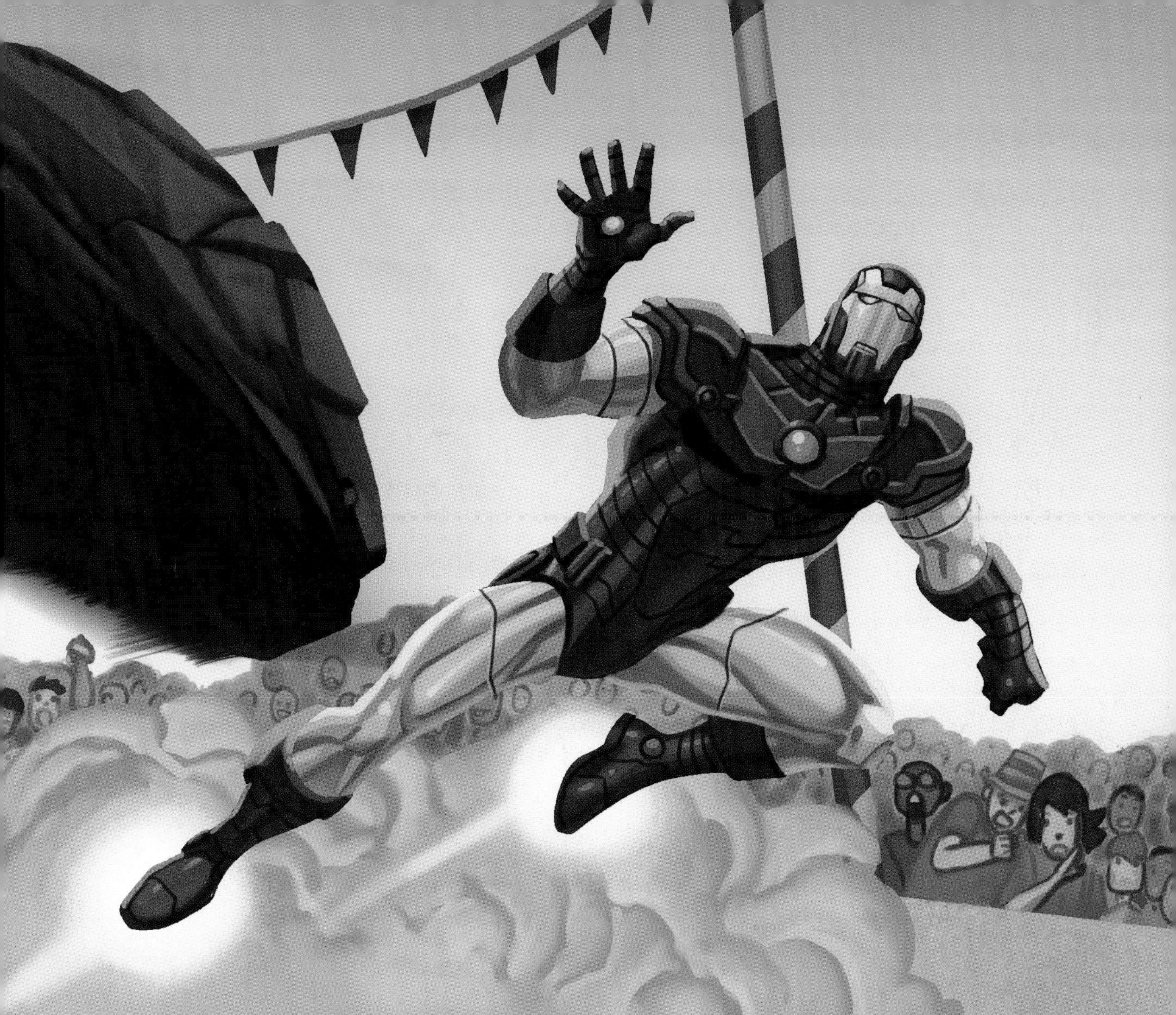

"I will show everyone who is more powerful!" Titanium Man shouted to the audience. The large super villain fired a beam that pulled Iron Man into his grasp.

"You're no match for my armor's tractor beam!" yelled the villain.

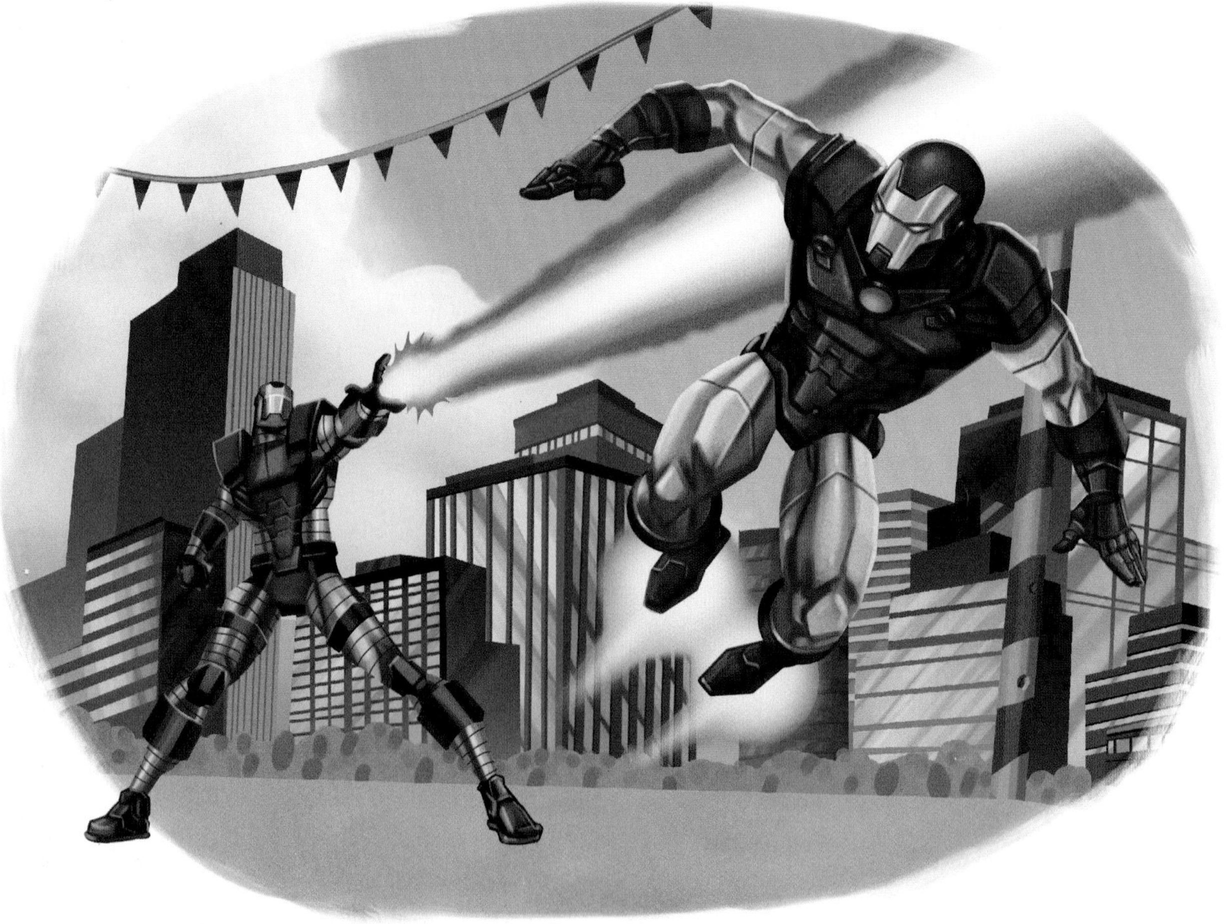

As the crowd watched, Pepper looked over at Happy and whispered, “This wasn't supposed to be a fight!”

“Don't worry, Pepper, Iron Man can handle anything,” Happy replied.

Iron Man fired his boot jets and managed to break free from Titanium Man's tractor beam!

"You can't escape from me!" Titanium Man laughed.

"Tony should really be here! Iron Man is fighting for his life!" Happy cried.

Tony noticed his friends searching for him in the audience. They did not know he was really Iron Man!

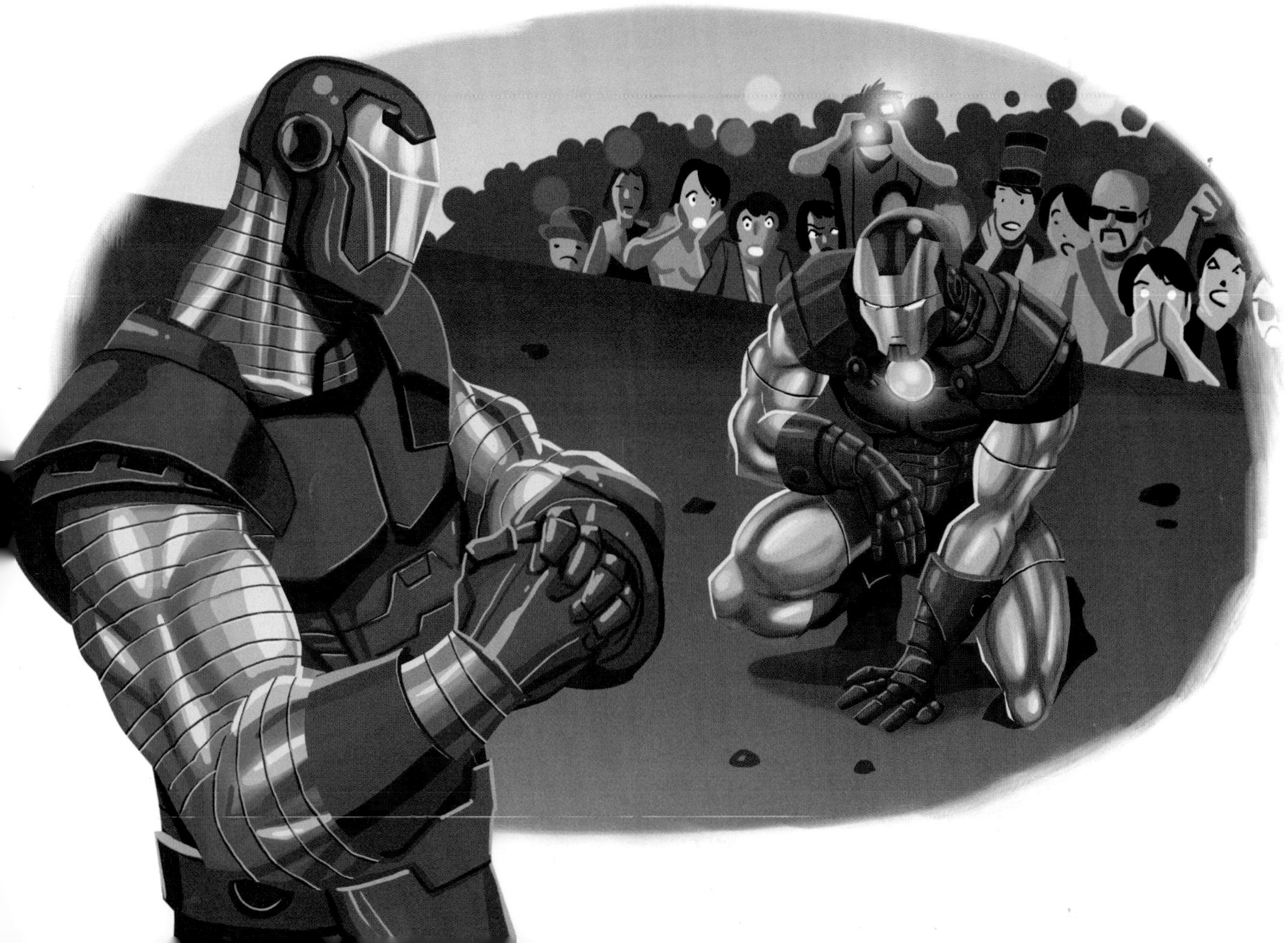

Power rings sprang from Titanium Man's palm and wrapped tightly around Iron Man's body.

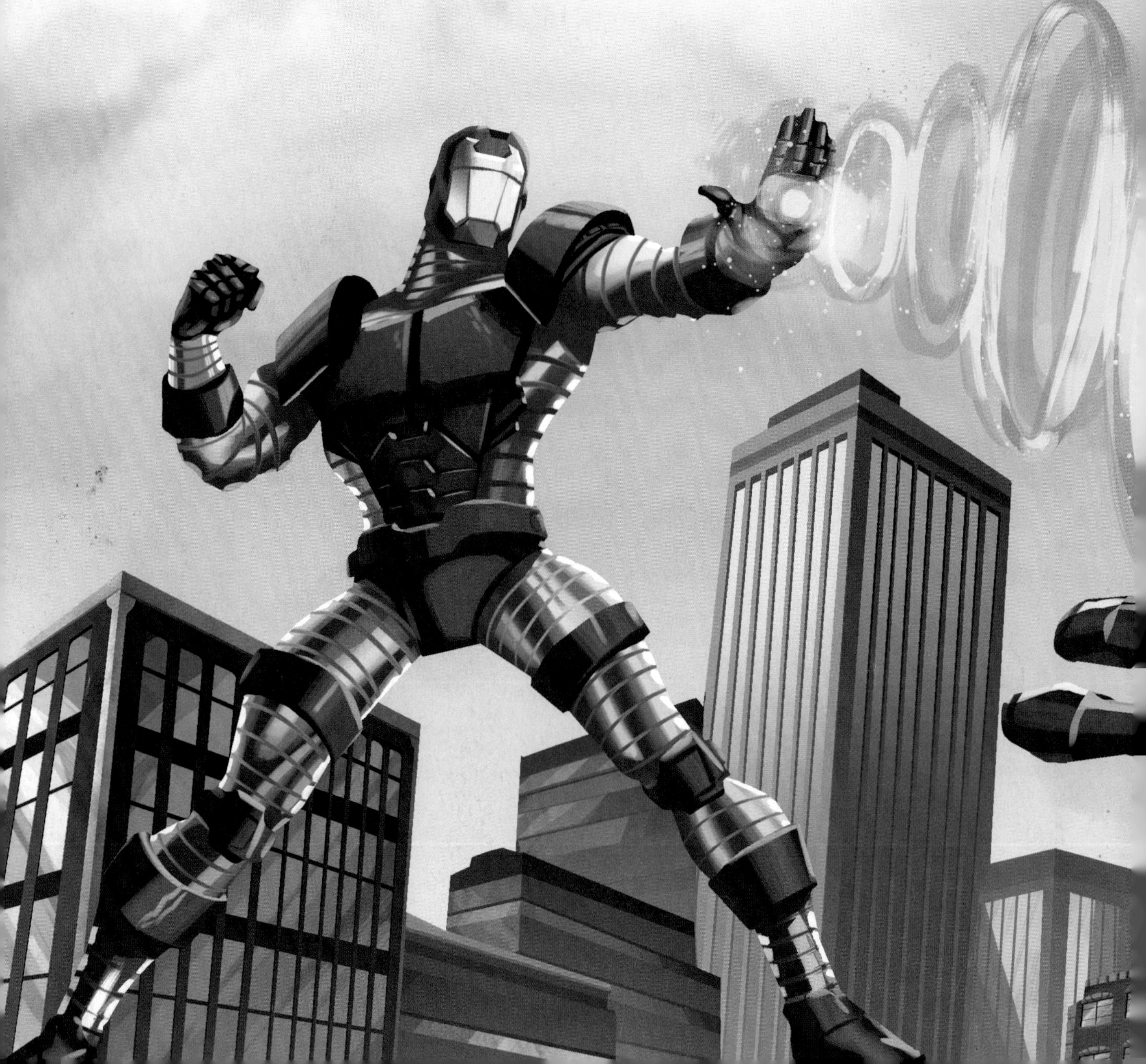

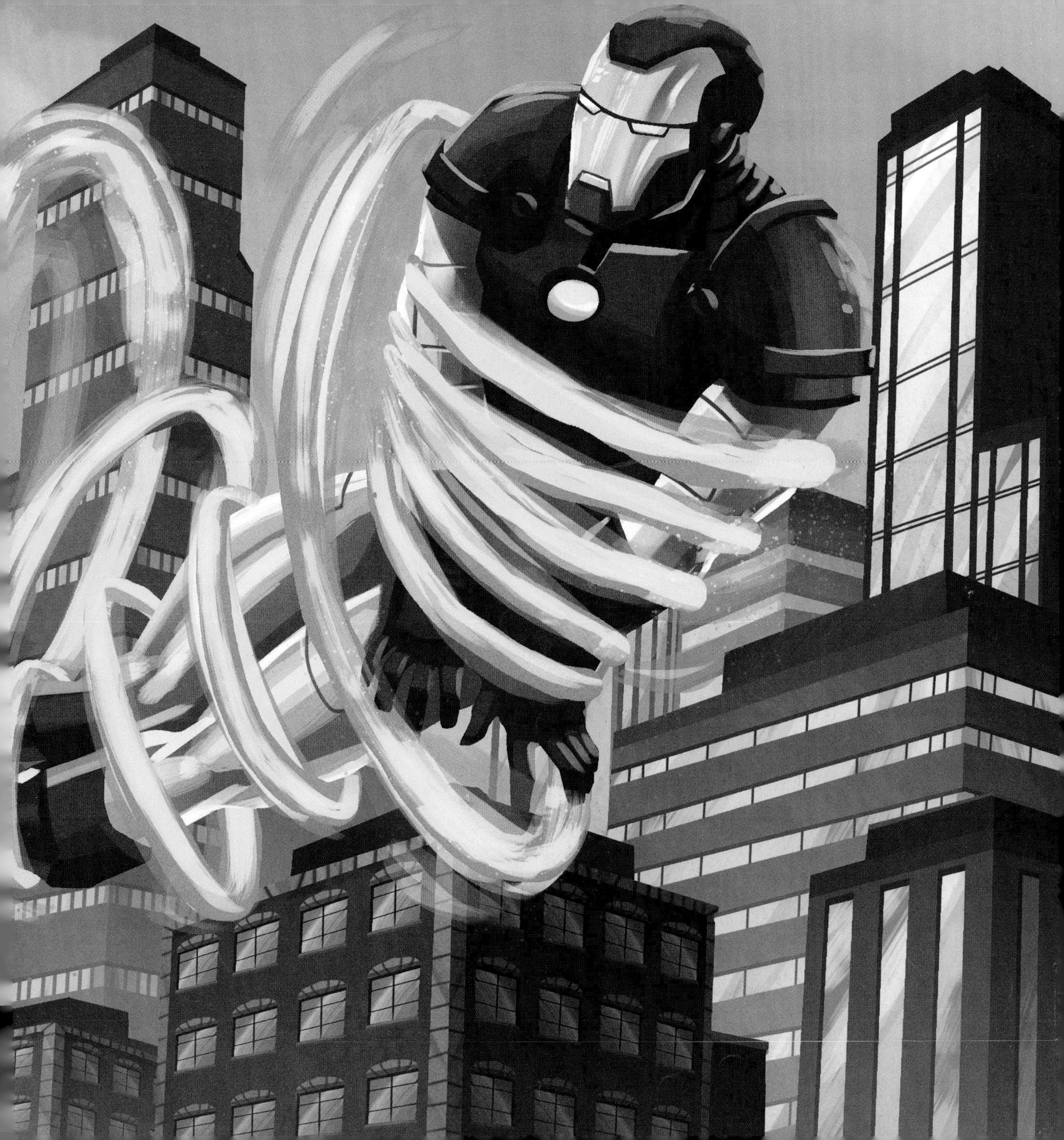

Iron Man struggled. But it was no use. Titanium Man floated above Iron Man's trapped form.

"Now, for the final blow. **My power-sapper beam!"** Titanium Man laughed.

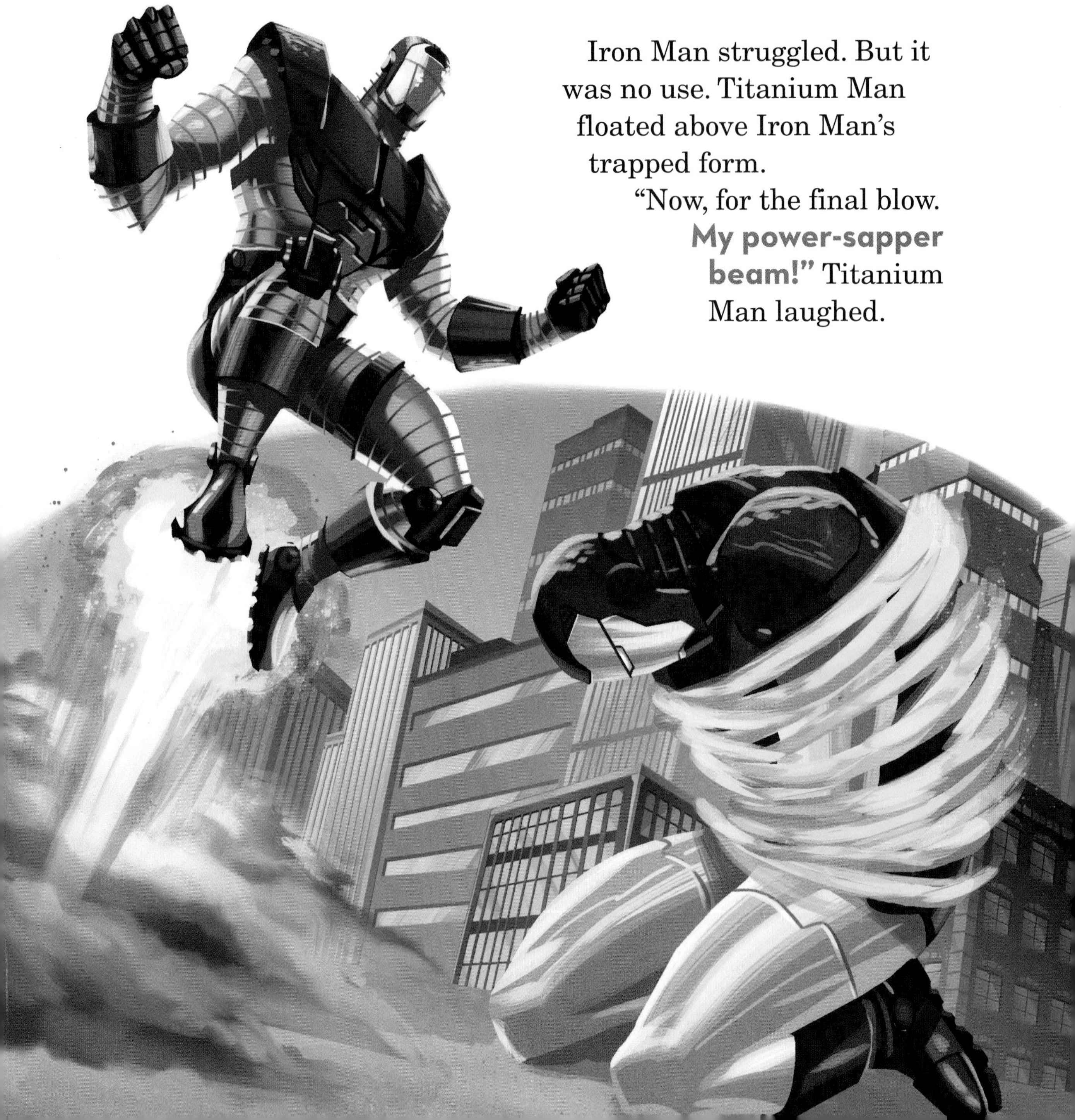

Iron Man fought with all his might and could slowly feel the rings loosening their grip! Suddenly, his armor's communicator told him someone was calling Tony Stark. It was **Pepper!**

"Tony! You have to come right away! Iron Man is in trouble!" Pepper shouted.

"I wouldn't count him out just yet," Tony said before hanging up.

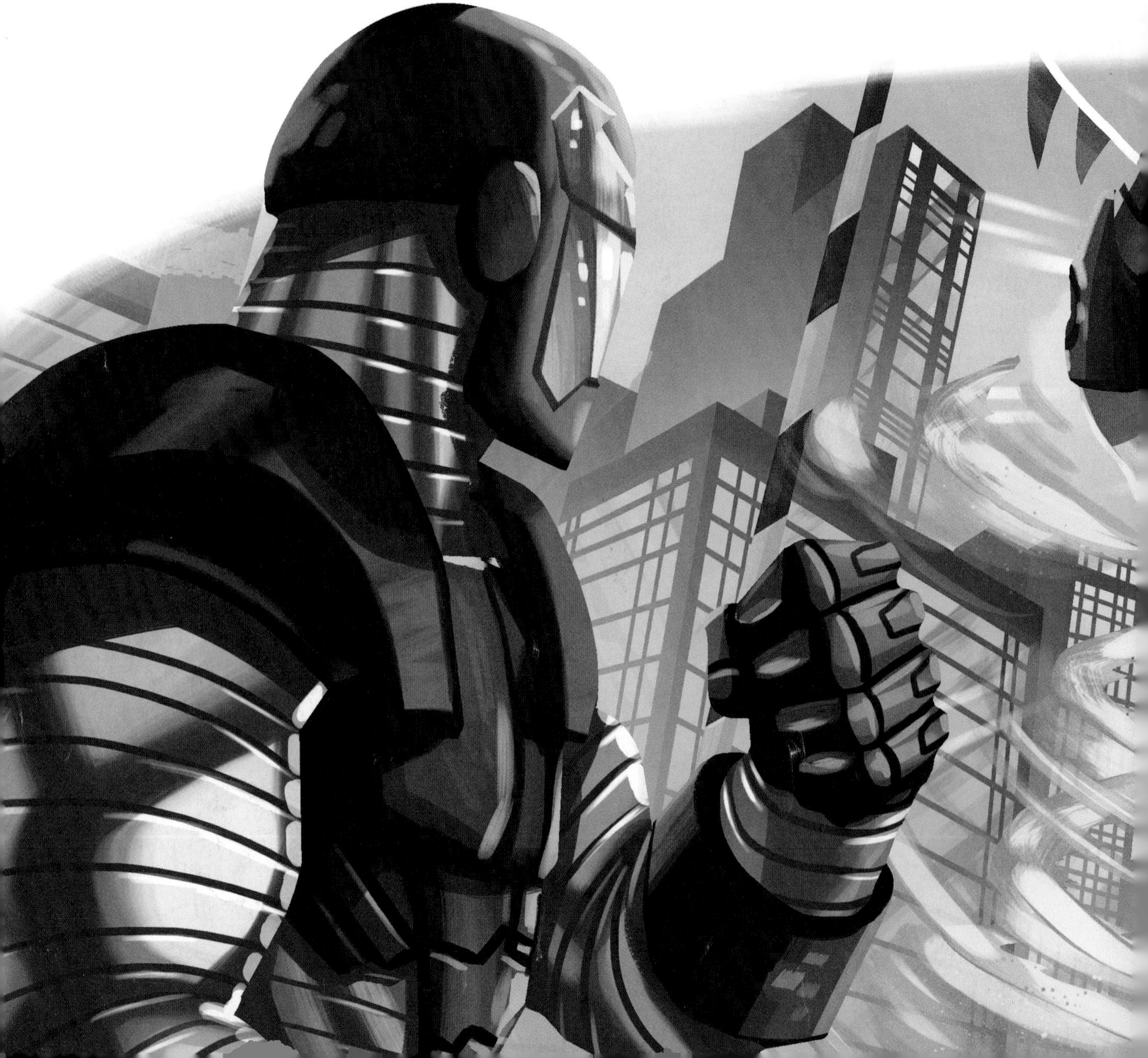

Iron Man used his reserve power to boost his strength. He was able to crack the power rings, **breaking free!**

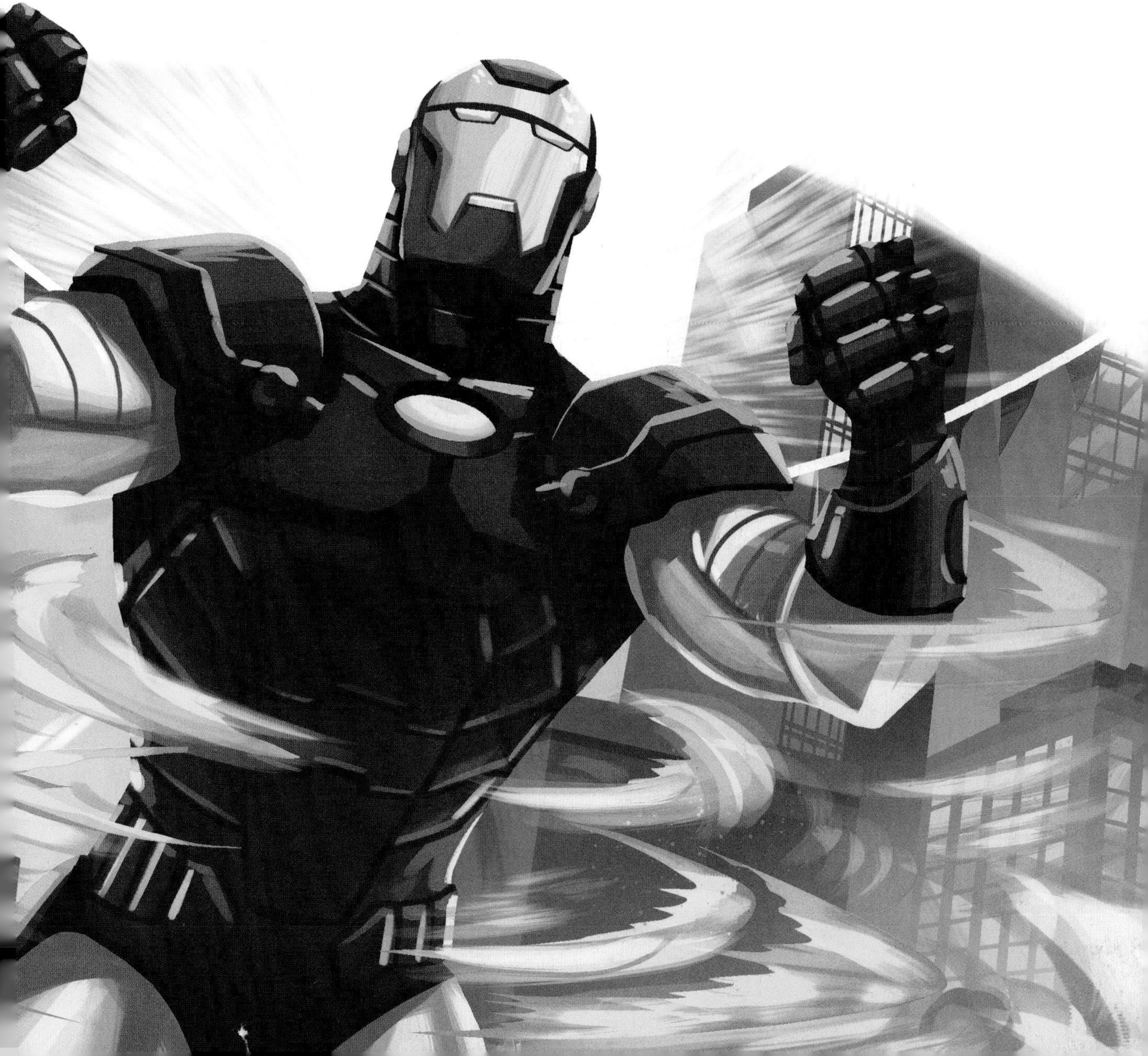

“I’m tired of your tricks,” Iron Man shouted as he flew at Titanium Man.

“I’m not!” Titanium Man threw another large boulder at the hero. Iron Man easily blasted this one to bits. But underneath **the rock was a trap.** An explosion went off!

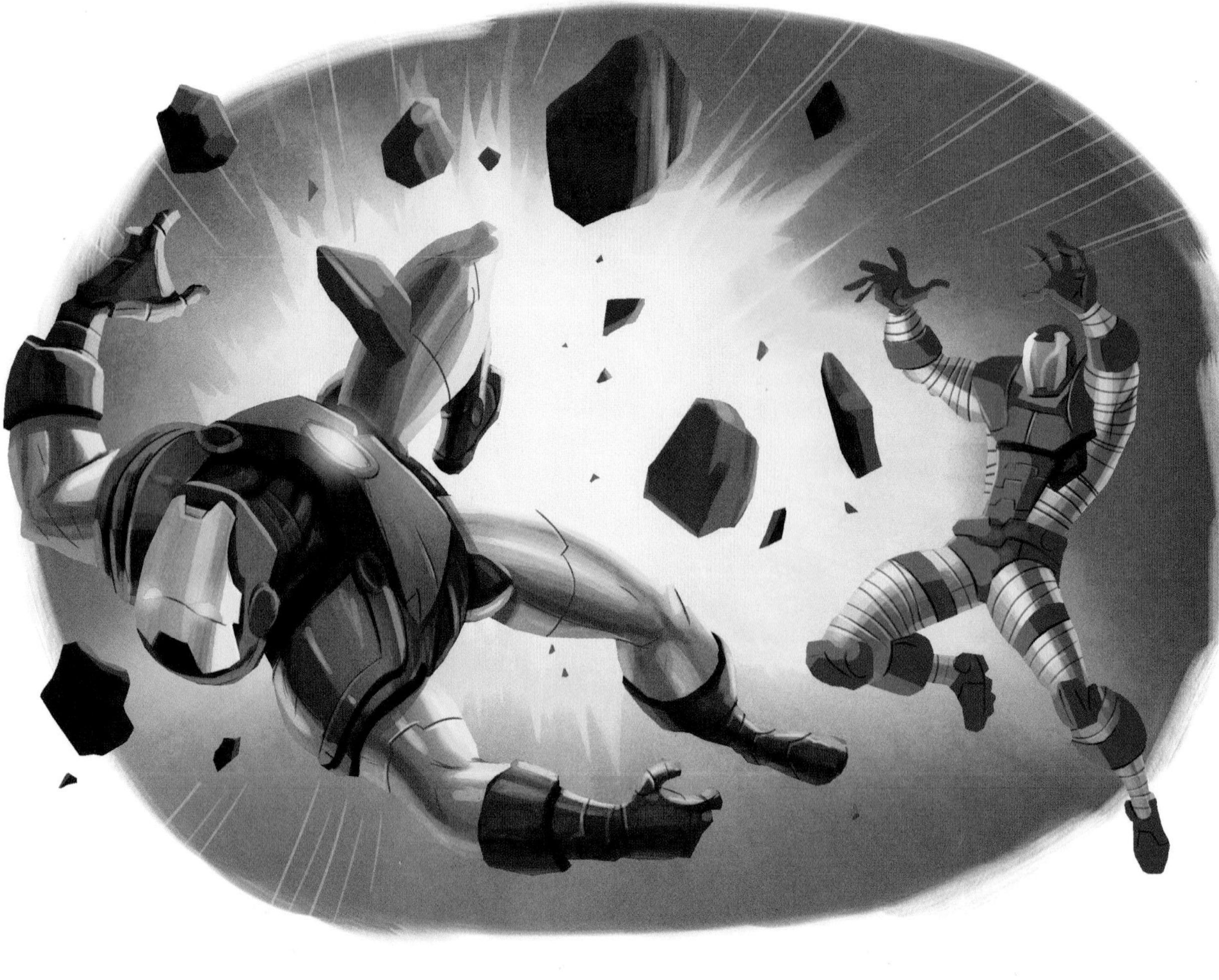

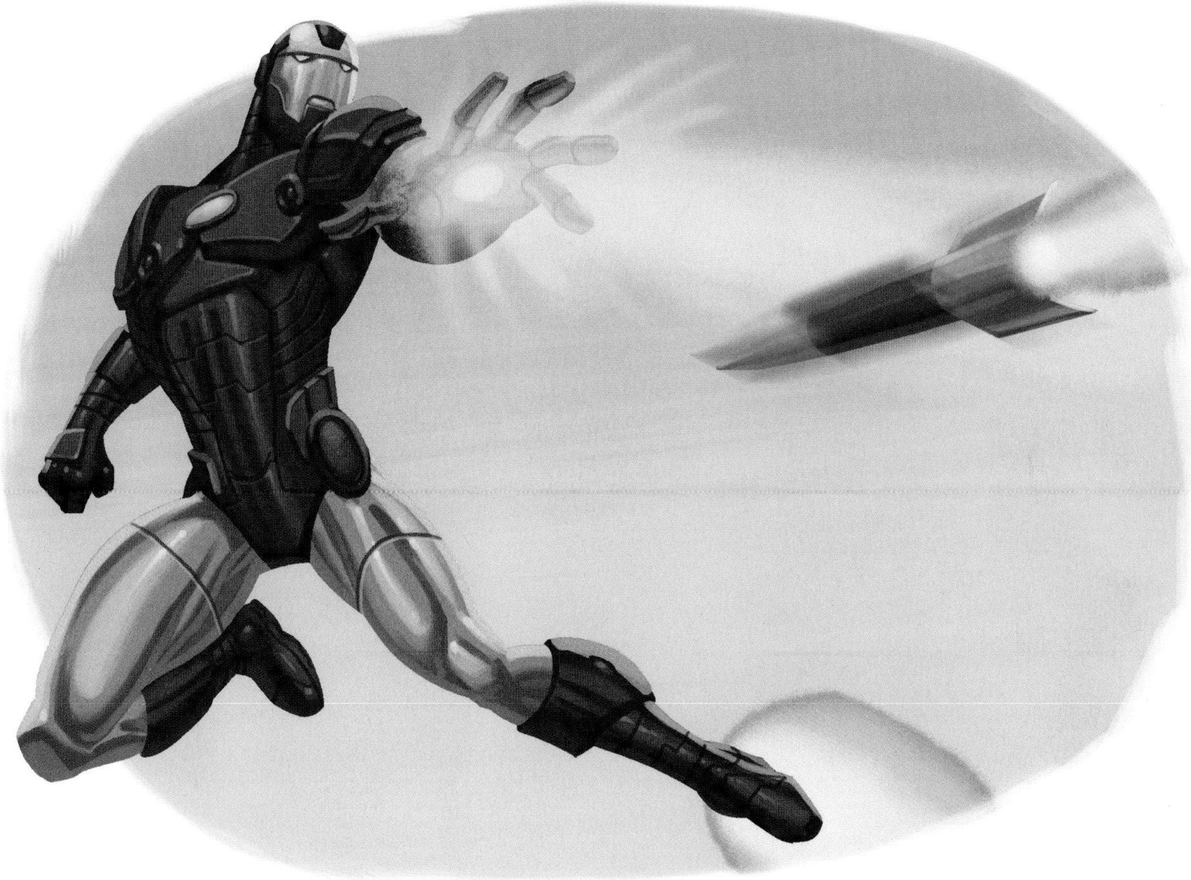

Titanium Man fired a rocket at Iron Man to try to finish him off.

Iron Man knew there was only one thing that could stop the rocket and Titanium Man: **his fire blast ray.** But even if it worked, he would have barely enough power left to stand up.

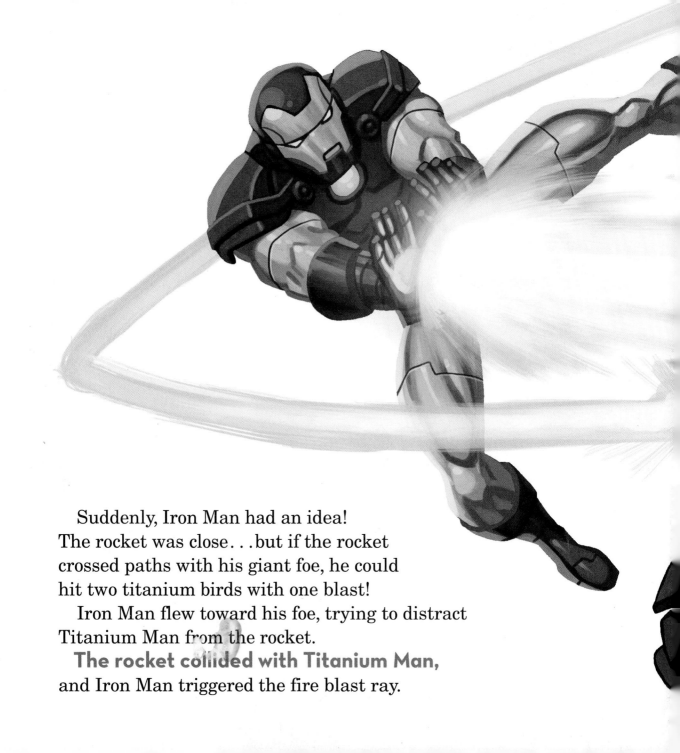

Suddenly, Iron Man had an idea!
The rocket was close...but if the rocket
crossed paths with his giant foe, he could
hit two titanium birds with one blast!

Iron Man flew toward his foe, trying to distract
Titanium Man from the rocket.

The rocket collided with Titanium Man,
and Iron Man triggered the fire blast ray.

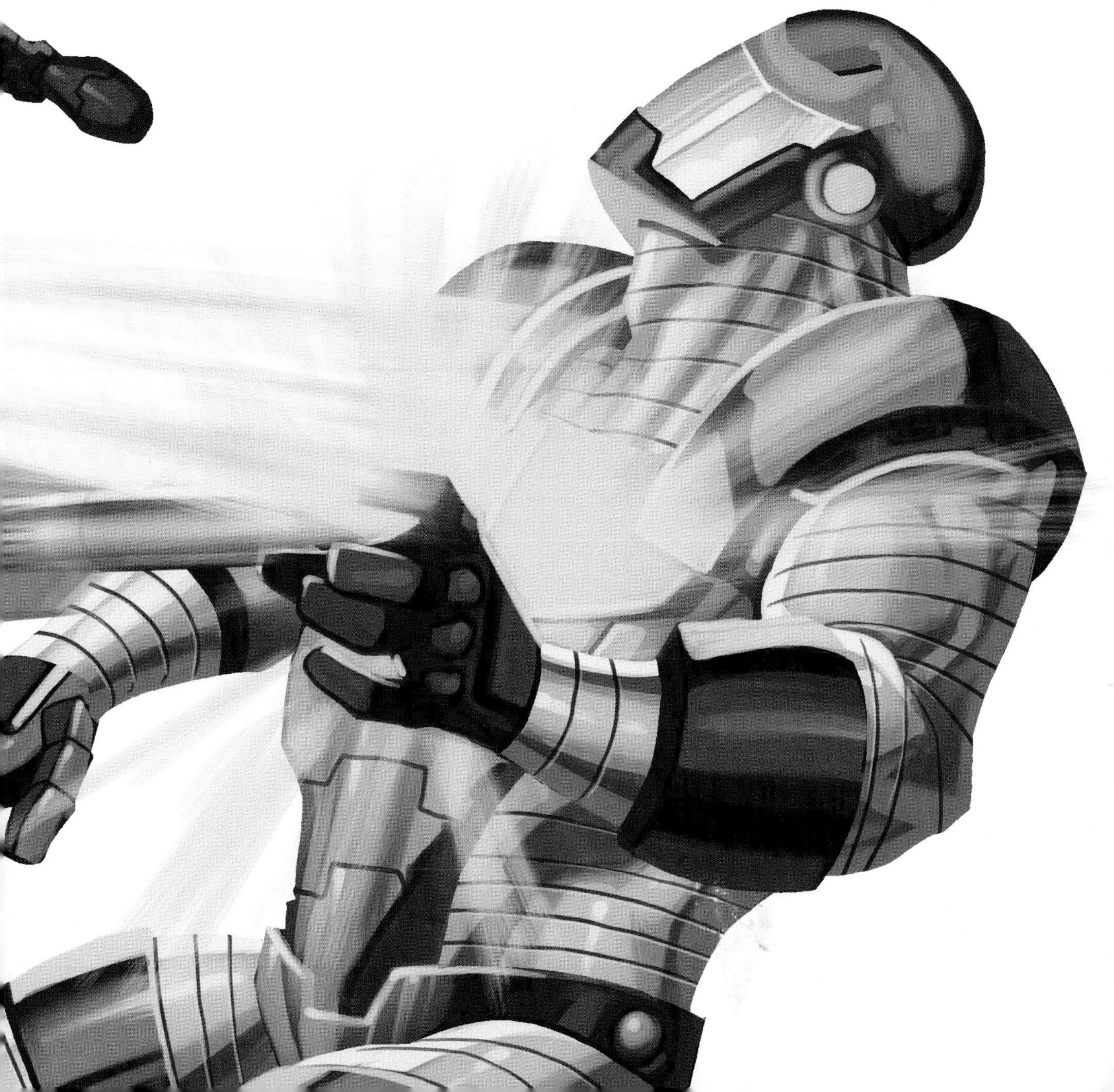

Dust and smoke clouded the area. It was hard to tell if Iron Man was successful. The crowd gasped. Pepper and Happy immediately rushed to the scene. Had both armored titans fallen?

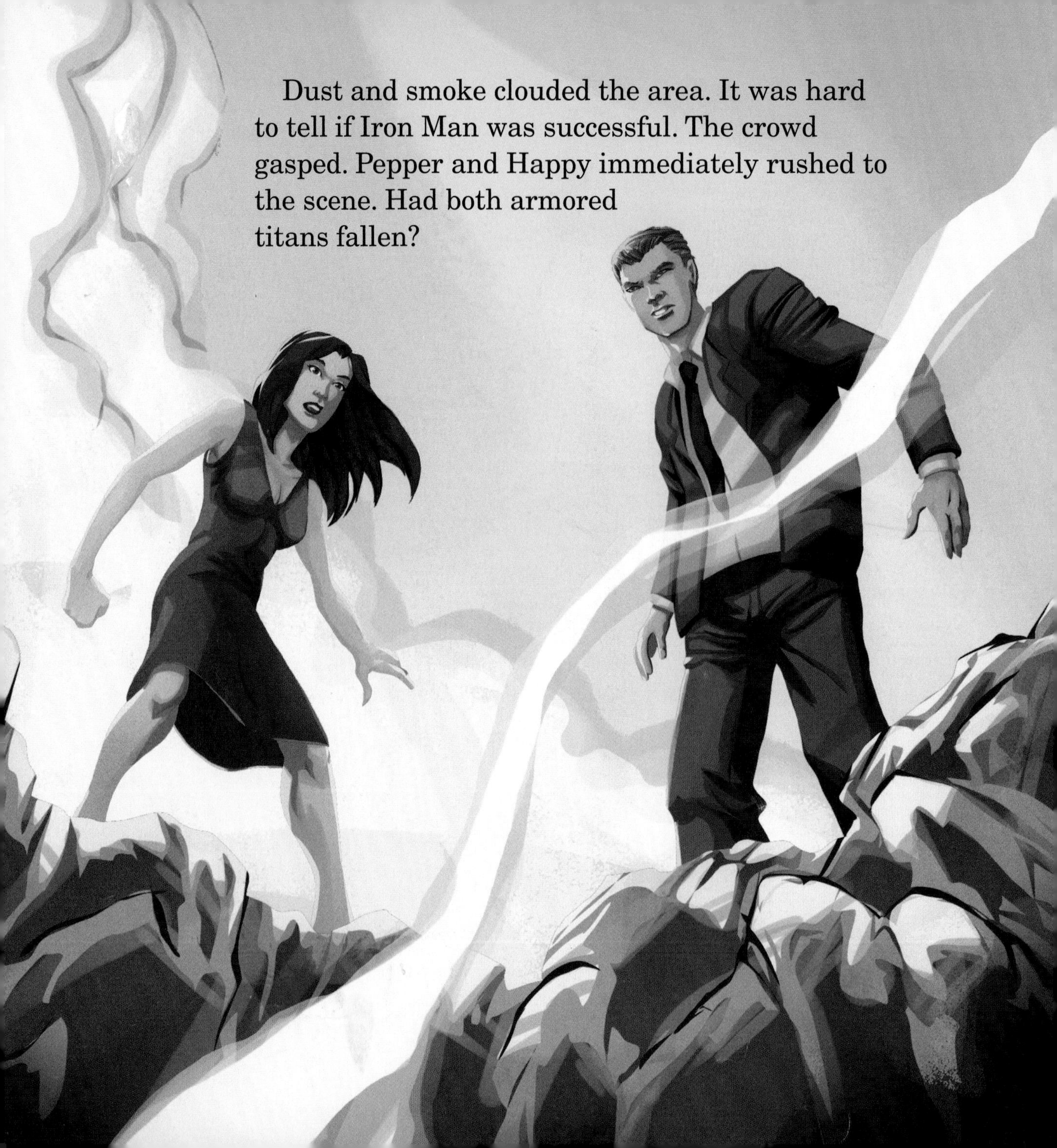

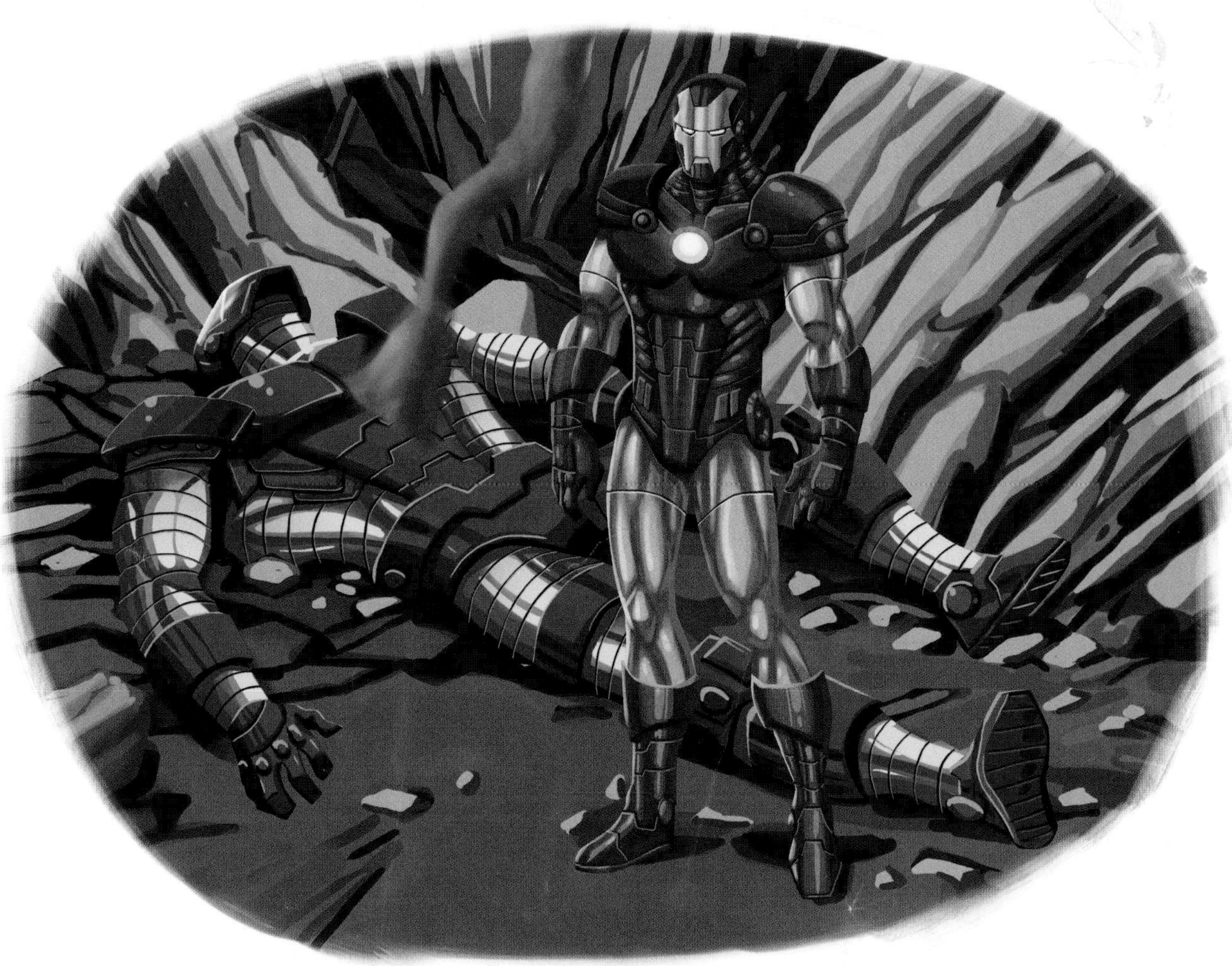

As the air cleared, Titanium Man lay motionless on the dirt in the shadow—the shadow of the Invincible Iron Man! Iron Man's armor had taken a beating. But **Iron Man had won! He had beaten Titanium Man!**

The people on the street cheered! The Invincible Iron Man had faced a dangerous and surprising foe, but underneath his helmet, Tony smiled. It was a great day for both Iron Man and Tony Stark!

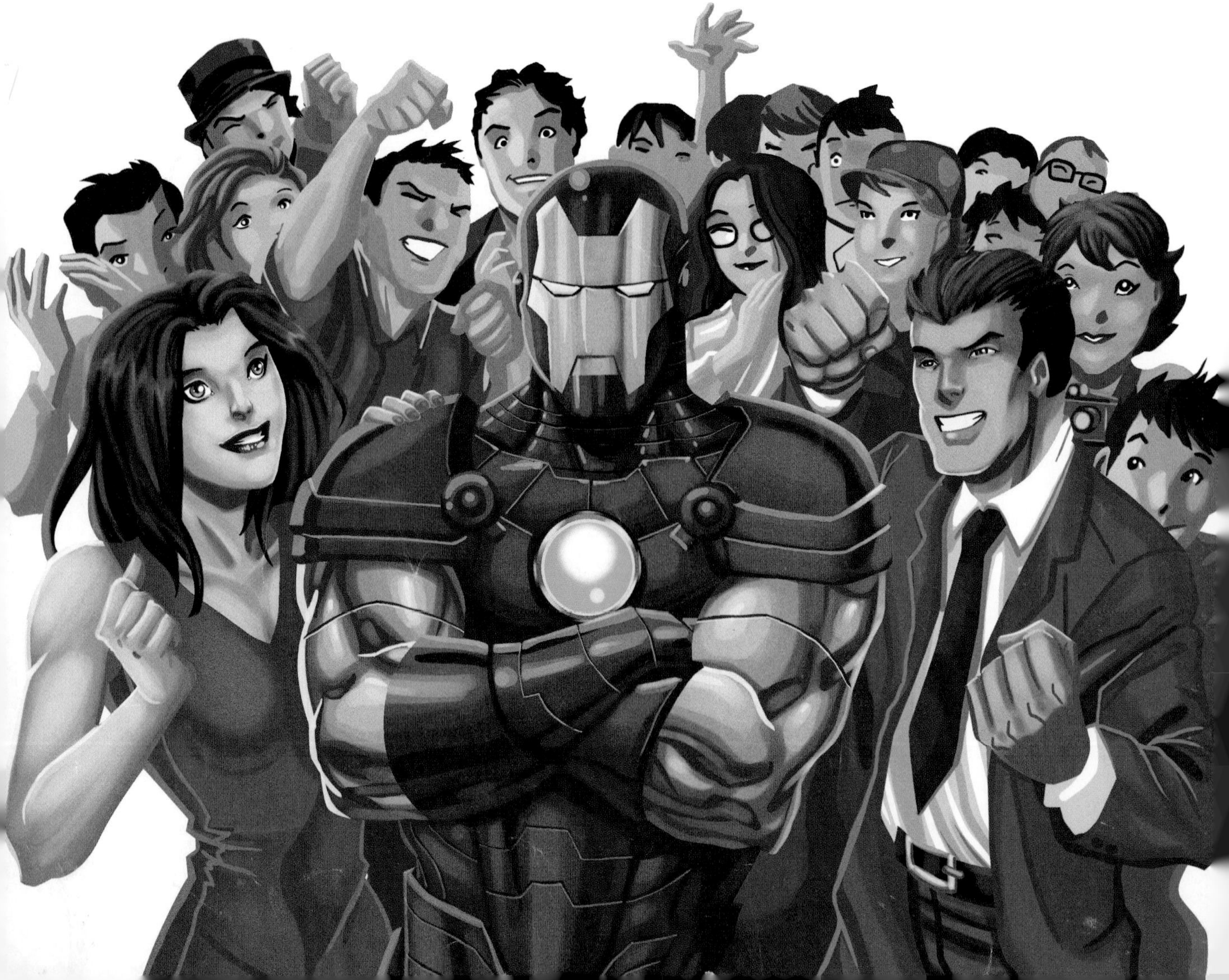